Mom and Mum are getting Married!

Written by KEN SETTERINGTON

Illustrated by ALICE PRIESTLEY

Second
Story
Press

You should have seen her.

Mom was dancing around the living room. In the afternoon. On a school day!

Nobody else was with her. There wasn't any music. But she wore the biggest smile I ever saw.

"What're you doing?"

Mom picked me up and started dancing again. "Rosie, I'm so happy, I'm almost as happy as the day you were born. That was my best, perfect day."

"Is another baby coming?"

"No, Mum and I are getting married!"

"Married, like a wedding? How come? Why can't we stay the way we are? I like us like this."

"We really want to celebrate how happy we are together — and we want everyone we love to celebrate with us."

"Well, okay, I guess." Then I remembered — "Hey, Mom, Jessica was a bridesmaid at her dad's wedding. Can I be a bridesmaid? Can we have tons of flowers? And a great big cake?"

"No, honey. We just want a small wedding."

"Not even one little bridesmaid?"

What was wrong with bridesmaids anyway? Rats!

Hey! Maybe I could be a flower girl. I started practicing — walking down the aisle scattering flower petals. I would be perfect.

*M*um brought Jack home from preschool and invited Nana and Pop for supper.

Nana hugged Mom. She hugged me, too. Then she tried to pick up Jack — "Ooooff!" — and put him down again. "This is so exciting! I'll have to get a new dress, and —"

"Nana, wait a minute," said Mom. "This isn't going to be a big splashy wedding, just a simple one."

Hmmm. Do simple weddings have flower girls? I wondered.

We talked about weddings while we ate supper. Nana told everyone how Pop sneezed all through their wedding ceremony.

"Did you have a flower girl?" I asked.

"No, dear," she replied.

Pop was full of questions. "Who will we invite? Where will we have it? Should we get —?"

"Stop!" Mum said it so loud she looked surprised. Then she blushed. "We want a simple wedding, Pop. Just a Saturday party at the cottage. No fuss, nothing formal!"

Things were not looking good. It was time to tell my joke.

"Why did the flower girl ride her bike to the wedding?"

Everyone looked puzzled.

"Because they needed lots of pedals. Get it? Pedals, petals."

No one laughed except Jack, but everyone smiled.

Mom's smile was sort of sad. Guess that meant no flower girl.

Then I had an idea. "Are you going to have rings? Someone always carries the rings. Jack and I can do that!"

"Jack's too little," said Mum.

"We'll practice, I promise."

Mom looked doubtful.

"We'll practice and practice and practice."

"You really want to, don't you?" said Mum.

Mom smiled. "Well, maybe when you're carrying the rings, you could scatter a few petals, too. But no bikes, okay?"

I pretended I wasn't sure and said, "Let me think about it."

Then I shouted, "YES!"

I got new shoes and a beautiful dress. Jack got a T-shirt with a suit painted on the front. Nana said she'd make lunch and Pop would make his super double-chocolate-with-extra-thick-icing-and-flowers cake.

We went to the cottage on Friday. I made Jack practice scattering petals and carrying rings made of grass. But Jack only wanted to pick the scab on his knee. "C'mon, Jack! One more time."

He ran off to the tree swing instead.

"What did you do with the ring, Jack?"

He pointed to where he'd been sitting. I'd never find it in all that grass. Maybe he *was* too little.

On Saturday everyone got up early, but I was already awake, worrying. What if Jack dropped the real ring?

Mum was finishing fixing my hair when people started arriving. First came Uncle Martin, then Auntie Wendy and Uncle Gerry with Maddy, Julian and Emily. Meema drove up in her old pink convertible. Soon there were lots of guests.

Uncle Peter came with Mike — they own a flower shop and brought tons of flowers. "Don't you look pretty," Uncle Peter told me. "I brought special petal baskets." He took a flower out of a basket and put it in my hair. "Now you're perfect!"

Mom looked beautiful but worried.

"Honey, I know we said you two could carry the rings, but I'm afraid Jack is going to lose his. Maybe Mum and I should carry them ourselves."

"Okay," I said, even though I really wanted to carry one myself.

Mom and Mum each took a ring and tucked it away carefully.

But a few minutes later, Mum asked me, "Did you give me the ring?"

"Yes."

"Are you sure?"

"Yup."

Mom added, "She did."

"Oh no! Where did I put it?"

Mum was definitely getting upset.

"It's in your little pocket, Mum."

She tried the wrong pocket.

"No, the other one," I said, pointing.

"Oh, honey, I'm so nervous I forgot. I'm sorry. I'm just afraid I'm going to lose it."

"I have an idea. Give me the rings," I said. "Uncle Peter, I need your help." I whispered my plan in his ear.

Mum and Mom looked confused.

"We'll be right back!" Uncle Peter shouted as we ran off with the rings.

In no time, Uncle Peter and I had done it! Jack and I each had a basket filled with petals. And in each basket there was a perfectly wrapped little present, tied to the handle with a bow.

Mom and Mum smiled.

"Jack would never lose a present," I said, "and neither would I."

"You are one smart girl." Mom didn't look worried anymore.

"Hey!" said Mum. "Let's get married! Start scattering those petals!"

Jack and I were supposed to scatter the flower petals on the ground, but Jack got so excited he began to throw them into the air. Everyone laughed, so I threw petals into the air, too.

Then Jack and I gave Mum and Mom our baskets. They unwrapped the rings and put them on each other's finger. Then they kissed.

Pop shouted, "Congratulations!"

Mike shouted, "Hurrah!" and all the guests clapped.

Uncle Peter handed me a bubble wand. Everyone else had wands, too,

but I got to blow the first bubbles. Soon there were bubbles everywhere.

Then Mum and Mom carried Jack and me through the bubbles to lunch. Everyone ate Nana's wonderful lunch and Pop's special cake.

"A perfect day," said Mom.

"The best," said Mum.

*A*fter lunch, Mom and Mum and Jack and me skipped over to our car. Mike had covered it with blossoms.

Uncle Peter said, "You can never have too many flowers."

"Or flower girls!" I shouted, and jumped into the back seat.

To Emily, Julian, Maddy and Rosie who carried the rings.

— K.S.

For Carter and Katerina Cook.

— A.P.

The author wishes to acknowledge the support of the Ontario Arts Council.

Library and Archives Canada Cataloguing in Publication

Setterington, Ken
Mom and mum are getting married / Ken Setterington ; illustrated by Alice Priestley.

ISBN 1-896764-84-3

1. Same-sex marriage--Juvenile fiction. I. Priestley, Alice II. Title.

PS8587.E835M65 2004   jC813'.6   C2004-903418-9

Text copyright © 2004 by Ken Setterington
Illustrations copyright © 2004 by Alice Priestley
First published in the USA in 2005

Edited by Charis Wahl
Designed by Laura McCurdy
Printed in China by Everbest Company Ltd.

Second Story Press gratefully acknowledges the support of the Ontario Arts Council and the Canada Council for the Arts for our publishing program. We acknowledge the financial support of the Government of Canada through the Book Publishing Industry Development Program, and the Government of Ontario through the Ontario Media Development Corporation's Ontario Book Initiative.

ONTARIO ARTS COUNCIL
CONSEIL DES ARTS DE L'ONTARIO

Canada Council   Conseil des Arts
for the Arts   du Canada

Published by
Second Story Press
720 Bathurst Street, Suite 301
Toronto, Ontario, Canada, M5S 2R4

www.secondstorypress.on.ca